HIGH SCHOOL MUSICAL

Written by Melanie Zanoza • Illustrated by Art Mawhinney

Based on the Disney Channel Original Movie "High School Musical," Written by Peter Barsocchini
Based on the Disney Channel Original Movie "High School Musical 2," Written by Peter Barsocchini
Based on Characters Created by Peter Barsocchini

© 2008 Disney Enterprises, Inc. All Rights Reserved.

Published by Louis Weber, C.E.O., Publications International, Ltd.
7373 North Cicero Avenue, Lincolnwood, Illinois 60712
Ground Floor, 59 Gloucester Place, London W1U 8JJ

Customer Service: 1-800-595-8484 or customer_service@pilbooks.com

www.pilbooks.com

Manufactured in USA.

p i kids is a registered trademark of Publications International, Ltd.
Look and Find is a registered trademark of Publications International, Ltd.,
in the United States and in Canada.

8 7 6 5 4 3 2 1

ISBN-13: 978-1-4127-7683-7
ISBN-10: 1-4127-7683-X

It's New Year's Eve, and it seems Troy and Gabriella have just started something new themselves. Sing along to their duet as you look for these party hats and favors in the crowd.

Noisemaker

Crown

Tiara

Pointy hat

Viking helmet

Horn

Top hat

Boa

WILDCATS

Gabriella and Troy's hobby has prompted a few other secret confessions. Look around the cafeteria for these Wildcats who refuse to stick to the stuff they know.

Zeke

Basketball-dribbling cheerleader

Cello-playing skater

Motorcycling student

Martha

Break-dancing guy

East High is buzzing with excitement — Troy and Gabriella got the leads in the musical, and the Scholastic Decathlon and basketball teams both won! Look around the crowded gym for these celebrating Wildcats.

Troy

Gabriella

Chad

Taylor

Sharpay

Ryan

Kelsi

What time is it? It's summertime, and the East High students couldn't be more excited! Can you spot these yearbook-carrying students looking for autographs?

School is out, but for most of the East High kids, that means summer jobs. As Ryan and Sharpay relax at their parents' country club, the rest of the Wildcats are hard at work there. Look around the kitchen for these things they'll need.

Troy's apron

Chad's order pad

Taylor's clipboard

Kelsi's sheet music

Zeke's toque

Gabriella's lifeguard whistle

Martha's cutting board

Jason's dishwashing sponge

The Wildcats performed in the Midsummer's Night Talent Show after all! After a smashing performance, Sharpay gives the Star Dazzle trophy to her brother, Ryan, for his great work directing the group. Can you spot his award, plus these other types of prizes?

Loving cup

Hollywood award

Blue ribbon

Gold medal

Giant check

Star Dazzle trophy

Basketball trophy

The Talent Show was a success, and now the kids can finally relax . . . at the pool party! Look around the sunny setting for one more glimpse of these Wildcats.

Gabriella

Troy

Chad

Taylor

Ryan

Sharpay

Groove your way back to the lodge party and look for these New Year's decorations.

Happy New Year!

Dribble back to the East High gym and look around for 26 basketballs.

The Wildcats are all in this together! Cheer your way back to the celebration in the gym and look for these examples of Wildcat pride.

WILDCATS!

E

EHS

Crowd your way back to the East High cafeteria and look for these familiar Wildcats as they learn a little more about their classmates.

Sharpay

Kelsi

Chad

Ryan

Troy

Gabriella

Taylor

Flip back to the last day of school and look for these abandoned school things in the crowded hall.

Troy doesn't work as a waiter for very long. Look around the kitchen for these items he will use after his promotion.

Italian golf shoes

Membership card

Tie

Golf club

Golf ball

Keys to his golf cart

Sharpay and her friends didn't perform the pineapple princess piece, but parts of their costumes ended up here somehow anyway. Can you spot these tropical things around the show?

Splash back to the staff party and look for these pool-party must-haves.

Ukulele

Sharpay's seashell headband

Pineapple headpiece

Ryan's seashell necklace

Lei

Tiki torch

Troy's lei crown